MAGICAL MONDAYS
AT THE ART MUSEUM

To Emily!
Happy Birthday! Enjoy
Birthday! Enjoy
the magic!
Kathe Reid

BY KATHLEEN REID

ILLUSTRATED BY ROBIN REIFSNIDER

Happy Birthday Emily!
May the magic of art
enhance your life!
Robin Reifsnider

COCKADOODLEDOO CREATIONS
RICHMOND, VIRGINIA

For my two girls with love. For my fantastic husband
and best friend whose support means everything to me. —KR

For my four precious ones who bring magic into my life everyday. . .
even on Mondays. And to the only one who keeps me
loose enough to enjoy the magic. —RR

We would like to offer a special thank you to Monica Rumsey.
She generously gave us her time, feedback, support, and
enthusiasm to make this project possible.

Graphic design by Lauri Mobley
Printed by Phoenix Color Corporation, Rockaway, NJ

Hardcover: ISBN 0-9702653-0-1
Paperback: ISBN 0-9702653-1-X

To order additional copies of this book, please contact *Magical Mondays*, PO Box 8653, Richmond, VA 23226
or Email: chaoswith4@cavtel.net

MAGIC IS FOR CHILDREN

As a docent for the Virginia Museum of Fine Arts, I understand the wonder each child experiences when he or she visits the art museum for the first time. Some children are a bit nervous at first not knowing what to expect. They carefully inspect each art object before asking questions. Others begin a gallery tour by demanding to know if they are going to see a real live mummy; they gasp in awe at life-sized statues of gods from other cultures or wall size paintings. By the end of a gallery tour, there is nothing like the wonder in each child's eyes when he or she ultimately connects with people and places from long ago. We would like all children to experience the magic of an art museum.

Since Magic is for children, we would like to help our community by donating a percentage of the profits from the sale of *Magical Mondays* to the Sacred Heart Center in Richmond, Virginia.

The Sacred Heart Center is a community center providing children and families in South Richmond with educational and social services. The Center's mission is to be a source of hope for the residents of Richmond's poorest and most troubled urban neighborhood. Working in partnership with a variety of community groups including The Junior League of Richmond, the Center provides a continuum of educational and care opportunities that are child-centered and family focused.

Robin and I hope that by sharing proceeds from the sale of this children's book with the Sacred Heart Center, we can give something a little extra to help those who are helping the youngest and neediest among us.

— KR & RR

FOREWORD

This book is meant to delight young children and to introduce them to the wonders at the art museum in Richmond, Virginia in a fun and creative way. Through the "magic" of fiction, many of the illustrations in *Magical Mondays* show the children interacting with the art works, but we want you to know that this museum, like most museums, has one very important rule for all visitors: Please do not touch the art. Many of the art objects are thousands of years old, and even the slightest fingerprint will leave a natural residue that, sooner or later, will harm the object's surface. Please help us preserve these precious objects for future generations of art lovers.

On Mondays, the art museum in Richmond, Virginia, like other museums, is usually closed. But once upon a time, on one special Monday, something unusual happened in the African Art Gallery. A statue of a rooster and a hen on a golden perch suddenly came to life.

"Wake up!" crowed the Rooster. "It's time to go to work. Cock-a-doodle-doo!"

Hen yawned and flapped her wings. "Oh my!" she cried. "The children are coming! The children are coming!" She clucked as she flew off the perch, calling out to her friends across the gallery:

**"IT'S MONDAY MORNING.
HERE WE GO!
WE HAVE HUNDREDS
AND HUNDREDS OF
OBJECTS TO SHOW.**

**IT'S GOING TO BE HARD TO
CHOOSE SEVEN OR EIGHT
BECAUSE EACH ONE IS
OH SO GREAT.**

**HOW ON EARTH CAN
WE DO IT ALL RIGHT,
BEFORE THE CLOCK STRIKES
TWELVE MIDNIGHT?"**

"Dear little Hen, stop worrying," said Rooster, shaking his head. "How did you get down off this perch so easily? My whole body's stiff from being frozen all this time! But I'm glad I finally get to talk!"

Hen looked up at him. "We have stories to tell and not much time. The children arrive at half past nine."

"Yes, and at least, they keep the temperature cool here to protect the art. When we served as the great storyteller's staff for our great chief back in Africa, I thought my feathers were going to fall off from the heat."

Hen began to think about their life together in Africa.

She smiled as she remembered the storyteller:

"THE LINGUIST TELLS STORIES THAT SPEAK
  FOR THE CHIEF—
STORIES OF FAMILY, KINSHIP AND BELIEF.

YES, HE IS THE ONE THEY WILL LISTEN TO
WHEN PEOPLE IN THE VILLAGE DON'T KNOW WHAT TO DO.

HIS PARABLE TELLS A SPECIAL KIND OF STORY
  ABOUT THE ORDER OF THINGS AND ABOUT THE CHIEF'S GLORY."

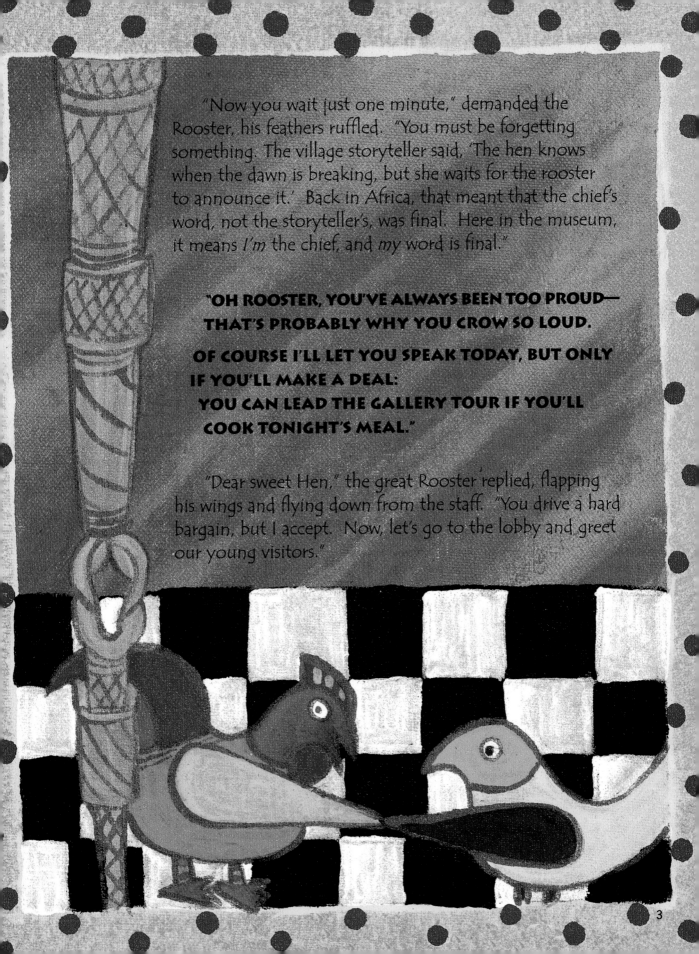

"Now you wait just one minute," demanded the Rooster, his feathers ruffled. "You must be forgetting something. The village storyteller said, 'The hen knows when the dawn is breaking, but she waits for the rooster to announce it.' Back in Africa, that meant that the chief's word, not the storyteller's, was final. Here in the museum, it means *I'm* the chief, and *my* word is final."

**"OH ROOSTER, YOU'VE ALWAYS BEEN TOO PROUD—
THAT'S PROBABLY WHY YOU CROW SO LOUD.**

**OF COURSE I'LL LET YOU SPEAK TODAY, BUT ONLY
IF YOU'LL MAKE A DEAL:
YOU CAN LEAD THE GALLERY TOUR IF YOU'LL
COOK TONIGHT'S MEAL."**

"Dear sweet Hen," the great Rooster replied, flapping his wings and flying down from the staff. "You drive a hard bargain, but I accept. Now, let's go to the lobby and greet our young visitors."

"Good morning children," said the Rooster. "Welcome to the art museum. I am delighted to be your tour guide today. We have so many wonderful pieces of art to show you. Have any of you ever been to an art museum before?"

Claire, Lily, and Jake raised their hands.

"Good. Then some of you already know that each work of art tells a different story. I'm a storyteller. Let me share those stories with you."

**"WE MUST BE GOING AND DO IT RIGHT
BEFORE THE CLOCK STRIKES TWELVE MIDNIGHT!"**

Rooster led the way to the Classical Court. "Please stop here and look at the beautiful things that may have been inside a home in ancient times."

"Those columns sure are tall," said Jake. "This room is bigger than my whole house!"

"Many of the buildings in the ancient world were created on a very big scale. These pillars are called Doric columns, the simplest kind used by ancient builders and architects. Let's take a moment and imagine what it must have been like to live in ancient Greece.

The ancient Greeks believed that gods and goddesses ruled their lives. The gods lived in a place in the sky called Mount Olympus. Zeus was chief of all the gods. His daughter, Athena, grew up to be the goddess of wisdom. The famous Greek city of Athens was named for her.

Now let's go meet the mighty Zeus and his daughter, Athena."

Rooster led the group into the Ancient Art Gallery and said, "See this tall vase — the Greek name is *amphora*, which means 'carried on both sides.'

The pictures that are painted on its sides tell one of the strangest stories in Greek mythology.

"Zeus learned that his wife, Metis, was going to give birth to a new leader of gods and men. Zeus was worried that the new king would steal his power. So to keep Metis from doing so, he swallowed her whole!

"Afterwards, Zeus became very sick and had terrible headaches. Hephaestus, the god of fire, opened Zeus's head to take the pain away. A new daughter, Athena, sprang forth out of his head, fully dressed for battle. The scene on the ancient Greek vase shows Hera, Zeus's second wife, and two other women helping with Athena's birth."

"What did the Greeks use the amphora for?" asked Lily.

"They used it on very special occasions to store drinks for their meals. Many people long ago — Greeks, Romans, and Egyptians — enjoyed many of the same things we do today, like good food and drink, music and dance."

"Now I get it!" exclaimed Jake. "You're saying that the ancient Greeks, who lived thousands of years ago, were like us in some ways. They were also different because they believed in gods and goddesses like Zeus and Athena."

"That's right!" exclaimed Rooster. "At the height of its power, Athens became a center for the arts where people from all parts of the Ancient World gathered to share ideas. The Greek city-states were well developed and later became part of the Roman Empire.

Some Roman emperors, however, were mean and cruel, and people feared them. Let's go look at a statue of a famous Roman emperor."

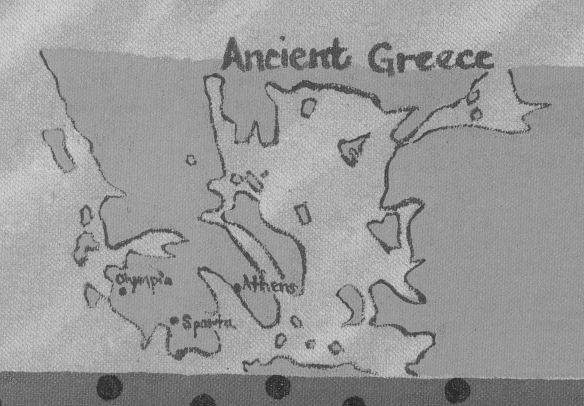

Ancient Greece

Olympia

Athens

Sparta

With a wave of his wing, colored lights flashed and the gallery magically became a stage for a game show. Claire, Lily and Jake took their seats.

Rooster announced, "It's time to play 'Who is the Real Emperor?' "

Suddenly, the curtain rose. The children laughed when they saw two figures — a life-sized statue, and Hen, wearing boots, perched on a pedestal.

"Meet Caligula, a Roman Emperor. His name means 'baby boots.' When he was a little boy, Caligula traveled around army camps with his father. Because he was little, the soldiers made a tiny pair of soldiers' boots just for him. This statue is one of only two in the world. Do you think Hen looks like Caligula with her boots on?"

"Of course not!" shouted Claire, Lily and Jake.

"No? Well, she may look more like Caligula than you think," said the Rooster, winking his red eye.

"What?" exclaimed Claire. "That doesn't make sense!"

Rooster rubbed his chin with his wing. "Historians found a description of Caligula that was written one hundred years after his death. It said that Caligula was very tall and extremely pale, with thin hair nearly gone and a forbidding face. This artist may have sculpted his statue to look like a god. Notice the traditional Roman toga. Caligula grew up to be a cruel man and he treated his people poorly."

"Why are there only two statues of Caligula in the world?" asked Jake.

"Good question," Rooster replied. "Caligula was so mean to his people that after his death, people either smashed his statues or put different heads on them."

Rooster walked over to the children. "It looks as if I have three winners here," he announced. "Now, we are going to meet a famous Egyptian."

"WE MUST BE GOING AND
DO IT RIGHT
BEFORE THE CLOCK STRIKES
TWELVE MIDNIGHT!"

With another wave of Rooster's wing, the stage disappeared. The children followed him to the Egyptian art collection.

"My young friends, I'd like you to meet Sema-tawy-tefnakht. ('Sema' for short). He was a very important man in his lifetime in ancient Egypt. You see, in his day, very few people could read and write, but Sema could. This man was a scribe for the Pharaoh, or King. If he lived today, he might be called Secretary of State. We know he was a scribe or secretary because he is seated and holds a roll of writing paper, called a papyrus scroll, across his lap. How many of you know someone who can read and write?"

"My mother or father reads stories to me every night," said Jake.

"Good! In our country, nearly everyone learns how to read and write. But in ancient Egypt, this was considered a very special job. We call Egyptian writing 'hieroglyphics.' Their alphabet had nearly 700 symbols and letters."

Suddenly, Rooster leaned closer to the Scribe. "Wait a minute! He has a message for us! Take a look at this, Hen!"

Hen read the scribe's words, then spoke them to the children in English.

"I AM, SEMA-TAWY-TEFNAKHT, A VERY IMPORTANT MAN
BECAUSE I ALWAYS TRY TO DO THE VERY BEST I CAN.

I CAN READ ORDERS AND I CAN WRITE RECEIPTS.
I WORK TO BUILD A BETTER WORLD AND THAT IS QUITE A FEAT.

MY JOB HELPS ME TO SERVE MY KING AND DO MY DUTY, WELL.
I WRITE ABOUT MY PEOPLE, THEIR GREAT STORIES I WILL TELL."

Rooster said, "Now that's one good leader! Let's go on to the
Indian Art Gallery to meet the God of Good Fortune."

"WE MUST BE GOING
AND DO IT RIGHT
BEFORE THE CLOCK STRIKES
TWELVE MIDNIGHT!"

As Rooster walked the group into the Indian Gallery, he stopped in front of a chubby statue with an elephant's head. "Meet Ganesha," he said, "the God of Good Luck or, as we say, Good Fortune."

"Why does Ganesha have an elephant's head?" asked Lily.

"There is a wonderful Hindu story about Ganesha," Rooster replied. "Long ago, Parvati, the Goddess of the Earth, needed someone to protect her. She used dust and water to make a child and named him Ganesha. She asked little Ganesha to stand outside her door to keep unwelcome people out. When the god Shiva came to visit, Ganesha refused to let him in to see Parvati. Shiva became angry and knocked off Ganesha's head. When Parvati found out what had happened, she was angry and demanded that Shiva do something to fix little Ganesha. Shiva said he was sorry and promised to replace Ganesha's lost head with the first thing they saw. As it happened, the first thing they saw was an elephant, and that's how Ganesha got his elephant's head! Shiva then made Ganesha 'Remover of All Obstacles,' the one to help people get what they want in life."

Hen clucked a song to his lovable god:

"AN ELEPHANT HEAD SHOWS GANESHA'S STRONG POWER.
AS A SYMBOL OF PEACE, HE HOLDS A LOTUS FLOWER.

GANESHA IS SEATED IN A POSE OF ROYAL EASE.
HE IS A KIND GOD, SO EAGER TO PLEASE.

THIS GOD IS RESPECTED AND LOVED BY ALL;
HIS ROUND BELLY SAYS HE LOVES CANDY — SWEET BALLS.

A MANY-JEWELED CROWN SITS ON HIS GREAT HEAD
WHILE A SNAKE HUGS HIS BELLY, GANESHA'S WELL-FED!"

"Well done, Hen!" Rooster crowed heartily. "Next, we're going to the Japanese Gallery, to see beauty with new eyes."

In the Japanese
Gallery, Rooster
pointed to a painting
hanging on the wall.

"How sad!" said Claire. "Look at that poor flower. Its petals are all
falling off. It's about to die."

"Claire," Rooster explained, "in the Japanese culture, a flower losing
its petals shows true beauty. The Japanese people hold great respect for
things that have lasted a long time, such as a flower that has bloomed
from the beginning bud until its last petal falls."

"That doesn't make sense," said Jake. "I always thought something
new was better than something old!"

Hen clucked and handed him two flowers. One was a new bloom, the other a wilted one. She said,

**"THIS FLOWER MAY BE A SYMBOL OF LIFE;
ITS JOY, ITS LOVE, ITS PAIN AND ITS STRIFE.**

**THE OTHER BLOOM IS PAST ITS PRIME;
IT HAS EXPERIENCED LIFE OVER A VERY LONG TIME.**

**IN JAPAN, BEAUTY IS NOT JUST FRESH AND NEW—
THE OLD BLOSSOM HAS BEAUTY FOR ITS AGE AND
WISDOM, TOO."**

Jake wrinkled up his face. "That sure is a different way of looking at things than what I always thought."

Rooster clapped his wings and paced across the floor. "True wisdom, my young friend, comes from both knowledge and experience. Perhaps now you can see how some other people think."

"Does this mean that my Grandmother Jane is more beautiful than anyone else in our family because she's older and has the most experience?" said Lily.

The Rooster's beak beamed a smile. "Precisely!"

**"WHEW!" HEN SAID, "WE NEED SOMETHING TO DRINK—
I GET THIRSTY WHEN ALL I DO IS THINK!**

**NOW IF YOU'LL JUST FOLLOW ME,
WE'LL TAKE A MINUTE TO STOP FOR TEA!"**

Rooster led the children to the "At Home" Gallery. He pulled a shiny silver teapot from the display case. He sat down at the table while Hen poured each of the children a cup of tea and offered them her special blueberry muffins.

"These are delicious," said Lily, sipping from her teacup.

Rooster pointed and said, "This teapot is made of silver, a most magnificent metal. It is called a precious metal because it is hard to get it from under the earth. There is only a small amount left, compared to other metals like iron."

"Who made this beautiful teapot?" asked Claire.

"A man named Paul Revere," Rooster answered. "Allow me to introduce you to him."

"Long ago, there was a French silversmith, Apollos Rivoire, who came to the New World to start a new business here. He even changed his name to Paul Revere. At that time, the people who lived here, in the British colonies, wanted to be able to stop paying taxes to the King of England. Revere taught his son, Paul Revere II, how to make beautiful silverware, like this teapot. Young Paul also learned to engrave designs into the silver. When the people decided to break away from English rule, young Paul Revere became a patriot."

"What's a patriot?"

"Someone who loves their country. Paul Revere loved freedom so much that he was willing to risk his own life for it."

The grandfather clock in the next gallery chimed.

"This teapot was made through a craft that has been done almost the same way for three hundred years. Now, let's look at some modern art and see what it teaches us about changing technology and newer ways of doing things."

Hen reminded them all:

WE MUST BE GOING AND DO IT RIGHT BEFORE THE CLOCK STRIKES TWELVE MIDNIGHT!"

In the Modern and Contemporary Gallery, Rooster stopped in front of a tall sculpture.

"What is it?" asked Jake, walking around the huge round shape.

"Can anyone guess?" said Rooster.

"Is it a wheel with hair?" asked Claire.

"No, try again," responded Rooster.

"How about an alien from another planet?" exclaimed Claire.

"It sure is strange looking," Lily whispered.

Rooster stepped forward. "Just twenty-five years ago," he said, "this object was used in daily life. It's called a typewriter eraser. Before computers were invented, people used to print their words with typewriters. Today, people press a button on the computer to erase a mistake in the computer's 'memory' before they print it out on paper. Back then, people printed words on paper and had to erase their mistakes by hand."

"Wow — that's a really big eraser," said Claire. "Why is it so big?"

"In the 1970s," Rooster said, "some artists made everyday objects larger than life, to show how much our world was changing, and how we were beginning to have too many machines in our lives."

"The time has come," Rooster announced, "when we must say goodbye. We have seen many different things, and I hope you now know more about how other people lived and thought in other times, and other parts of our world. Perhaps you can see how we are all a little bit alike, even though we live far apart in time and space.

The art that people make tells us a lot about them.

"We have seen that the gods were very important to the people of ancient Greece and Rome. We met Caligula and learned that he was not a good leader for his people. Sema-tawy-tefnakht showed us that it is still important to learn to read and write, as it was in ancient times.

"We know that the people of India love Ganesha. We learned about true beauty through Japanese eyes. We looked at a teapot by Paul Revere II, a patriot and silversmith. And a lowly typewriter eraser told us how much our world has changed and now depends on computers."

"Thank you all for coming," Rooster crowed.

"Can we come back next Monday?" asked Jake.

"And every Monday after that?" said Claire.

"Whenever you can," said Rooster with a knowing smile.

Rooster and Hen had done it right.

After the children left, Rooster said, "Sweet little Hen, you did a fine job, a very fine job. But I'm so tired, I could sleep for a week."

Hen looked sad.

**"YOU PROMISED ME A DINNER FOR TWO
IF I LET YOU GUIDE THE CHILDREN THROUGH.**

**I'D LIKE A CORNMEAL PIZZA WITH EXTRA CHEESE—
CAN YOU CALL FOR A SPEEDY DELIVERY, PLEASE?"**

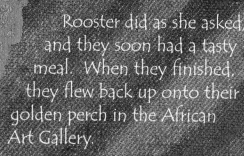

Rooster did as she asked,
and they soon had a tasty
meal. When they finished,
they flew back up onto their
golden perch in the African
Art Gallery.

Hen clucked happily,

**"WE DID OUR JOB WELL AND
WE DID IT RIGHT
AND ALL BEFORE THE STROKE
OF TWELVE MIDNIGHT."**

Just then, they froze in place,
just as you see them in the museum.
This time, Hen had the last word.
That night, they would both dream
of seeing more children the next
Monday, just after sunrise . . .

I Can Do It By Myself

Written by: Madison Stokes

Transcription by: Joseph Mcanulty, Aleah Watson, and Floyd Stokes

1. I can go to sleep my self   I can do it   by   my   self

2. I can wake up by myself
   I can do it by myself

3. I can brush my teeth myself
   I can do it by myself

4. I can comb my hair myself
   I can do it by myself

5. I can wash my face myself
   I can do it by myself

6. I can button my shirt myself
   I can do it by myself

7. I can beat the drum myself
   I can do it by myself

8. I can eat my food myself
   I can do it by myself

9. I can tie my shoes myself
   I can do it by myself

10. I can kick the ball myself
    I can do it by myself

11. I can ride my bike myself
    I can do it by myself

12. I can take a bath myself
    I can do it by myself

13. I can read my book myself
    I can do it by myself

I   can do   it   by   my   self   I   can   do   it   by   my   self